Wanda's Monster

WRITTEN BY

Eileen Spinelli

ILLUSTRATED BY

Nancy Hayashi

Albert Whitman & Company

Morton Grove, Illinois

Library of Congress Cataloging–in–Publication Data

Spinelli, Eileen.
Wanda's monster / written by Eileen Spinelli ; illustrated by Nancy Hayashi.
p. cm.
Summary: When Wanda fears that she has a monster in her closet, she takes her
grandmother's advice and begins to look at things from the monster's point of view.
ISBN 0–8075–8656–0 (hardcover)
[1. Monsters — Fiction. 2. Fear of the dark — Fiction.
3. Grandmothers — Fiction.] I. Hayashi, Nancy ill. II. Title.
PZ7.S7566 Wan 2002 [Fic] — dc21 2002001955

The illustrations were done in watercolor and Prismacolor
pencils, on hot press Lanaquarelle watercolor paper.
The design is by Scott Piehl.

For information about
Albert Whitman & Company,
visit our web site at
www.albertwhitman.com.

For Harriet Savitz and Susan Austin — E. S.

For Tom — N. H.

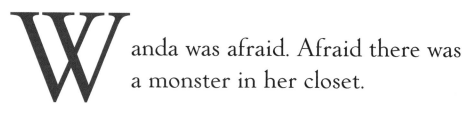 anda was afraid. Afraid there was a monster in her closet.

Dad brought his flashlight. He zigzagged the
beam across Wanda's dresses and shirts. Into her
empty rain boots and shoes.

"No monster in there," he declared.

"Nope, no monster," added Wanda's mom, mopping the closet thoroughly. She packed up some clothes Wanda had outgrown. "Little Cousin Ruthie can use these," she said.

Wanda's big brother snickered. "There's no such thing as monsters."

But when the others had gone, Granny came in. She sat on the edge of Wanda's bed and said, "There *could* be a monster."

Wanda's eyes grew big as quarters. "Really?"

Granny put her ear to Wanda's closet. She listened. She gave the door a tap with her elbow. She listened again. "Yep," she said at last. "I do believe there's one in there."

"Oh, no!" Wanda cried, and hid behind her
beanbag chair.

"'Oh, no' is right," said Granny. "How would *you*
like to live in a cold, dark closet?"

"I never thought about it," Wanda replied.

"Of course you didn't think about it," said
Granny. "Look at this room. Pretty wallpaper.
Flowered curtains at the windows. Toys. Games.
Books. Soft pillows. All that monster has to rest
his head on is an old rubber rain boot."

"But what does a monster care?" said Wanda.

Granny wagged her finger at her granddaughter. "See—that's the kind of attitude monsters have to deal with." She pointed to the closet door.

"Why do you think monsters hide themselves in closets and basements and attics and under beds?"

Wanda peeped, "Why?"

"Because they're *shy*; that's why."

That night Wanda went to bed, but she couldn't sleep. She couldn't stop thinking about what her grandmother had said.

At last, she got out of bed. She dragged one
of her pillows to the closet. She quickly tossed it
in and slammed the door. "There!" she said.

The next night she tossed in her panda bear.

Slam!

And the next night, a coloring book and a box of crayons.

Slam! Slam!

One night when she felt especially brave, she
gave the door a tap with her elbow and listened.

She almost thought she heard something.

Wanda began reading bedtime stories aloud.
"Here's one you'll like!" she called out. At first she
sat on the bed. Then on the floor before the closet.

She tried to choose stories that weren't too scary.

When she wrote her first poem, she recited it.
She opened the door just a crack.

When Aunt Sue brought little Cousin Ruthie over to help bake cookies, Wanda nudged a cookie under the door with a stick.

One day Wanda said to Granny, "I'm sort of getting used to that monster."

"Better not get too attached," Granny advised. "He'll be leaving next week."

"Huh?"

"Oh, yes," said Granny. "Monsters have rules, you know. They never stay in one closet for more than seventeen days and nights. Time's about up, I do believe."

Wanda felt an ache in her heart.

On the seventeenth day, a snowstorm howled
about the house. Wanda looked out the window.
"He can't go anywhere in this," she said to Granny.
Granny shrugged. "Monsters are *always* on
schedule."

That's when Wanda decided to give the monster her favorite scarf. The red one she had gotten for her birthday. Something to keep him warm.

She also decided to give him an address for his next visit, printed on a card. Someplace close by so he wouldn't have to trudge too far in the blizzard.

She put the scarf and the card in a box. She set the box in the closet. She blew a kiss into the darkness. "Goodbye," she whispered, and gently closed the door.

The next morning, Aunt Sue telephoned,
"Come quick—little Ruthie is screaming. She says
there's a monster in her closet!"
Everyone ran to Aunt Sue's.
Wanda's dad brought his flashlight.
Wanda's mom brought her mop.